T0065600

Eclipsing Death

The joy and horror that followed

Michael Neno

authorHOUSE®

AuthorHouse™ UK
1663 Liberty Drive
Bloomington, IN 47403 USA
www.authorhouse.co.uk
Phone: 0800.197.4150

Published by AuthorHouse 07/19/2016

ISBN: 978-1-5246-6102-1 (sc)
ISBN: 978-1-5246-6101-4 (e)

Print information available on the last page.

Any people depicted in stock imagery provided
by Thinkstock are models, and such images are
being used for illustrative purposesonly.
Certain stock imagery © Thinkstock.

This book is printed on acid-free paper.

Because of the dynamic nature of the Internet, any web
addresses or links contained in this book may have changed
since publication and may no longer be valid. The views
expressed in this work are solely those of the author and do
not necessarily reflect the views of the publisher, and the
publisher hereby disclaims any responsibility for them.

CHAPTER 1

For the second time it was the 12th August 1998 only this time Jane was alive and with me with our whole lives ahead of us after the magical occurrence during the full eclipse the day before and now due to happen again only 12 months later. After 1 spending a whole year feeling the pain of having the one I love more than anything killed in a tragic car accident and then returned to me, all I wanted was to thank God by allowing me to do something good with time being rewound a year to live again. With that, I was happy at knowing my love would be discovering that she was pregnant with the child that would have never be born if not for the magic of the full eclipse and Gods grace.

When I looked at Jane my thoughts straight away turned my attention over to how we could make the coming repeat of the previous year be a happier one than the one where she had been dead. Her just being alive again for me was more than I could possibly dream of yet she was and we had the gift of reliving a whole year. Before her accident during the day I would have gone to go to work filling the shelves in a local supermarket and Jane was due to meet her modelling agent about working with her best friend Lindsey, modelling for a travel agents before the following holiday season.

We kissed goodbye at the door before heading off in opposite directions, me for my motorbike and Jane to her car to go to our days work. I rode to the end of our road and turned left heading onto the one way shopping street past the turning toward the church where we had decided that we wanted to get married and the graveyard where she had laid to rest after her death, past the public house where Jane Lindsey and I would often unwind after a busy day's work with a drink and snack and finally past the turning into the police station where I had spent 24 hours and met John the police detective who had, questioned me the year before but about to be relived after Jane's body had apparently been exhumed and for which I had been held as a suspect.

For obvious reasons I tried not to show the joy in my heart on this particular day but all day long colleagues were asking why I was so happy with comments like "have you won the lottery and are you on happy pills." It felt quite unreal to me how on this day the year before I had been in hospital, feeling the trauma of an accident and loosing the girl I loved killed at my side, yet now it had never happened, even so I could not resist calling Jane just to tell her how much I loved her at lunchtime.

With the working day over I quickly returned home where Jane, having beaten me back, had cooked us a meal. After eating a simple meal of pie and mash potato she phoned her best friend to talk more about the day's meeting with their modelling agent, while I cleared the table before snuggling up on our couch to watch a movie and then turning in for the night. This was basically the way our lives were going, until on the 21st of that month, when at 7.30 in the morning we received an unexpected telephone call from John, the police detective who had arrested me over Jane's grave being dug up asking to visit us later that morning.

With a mixture of intrigue and nervousness by the phone call from John, one which was a total surprise to us both, Jane and I waited in our lounge awaiting him with trepidation and nervousness at what might be about to happen.

"How does he remember what happened before my death and then return to life?" asked Jane, clearly frightened at the possible consequences if made public knowledge.

At 11.45 in the morning John knocked at our door heralding his arrival, so with Jane standing sheepishly behind me, I opened it not knowing what to expect.

3

After giving the customary hello and welcome he held up a package and asked if he could come in and talk with us. Before allowing him to enter I looked over his shoulder to see if he was alone and we were not about to be inundated by the police. Apart from his parked unmarked private Honda civic car, there was not a sign of anyone so I beckoned him in, leading him into our lounge. He was wearing a pair of black casual trousers, a plain red sweat shirt and ordinary shoes which were not what one would expect from a police officer.

Leading the way I made a point of noticing how John was looking all around while seeming not to know where he was going, not having any knowledge of where he was now. "Do you not recognise us or our home John?" asked Jane clearly uncertain as to why he was there in the first place.

"Not as far as I know, do you know me?" but in light of the contents of the wrapped package he was carrying, for me to open that might change. I accepted it with hesitation and carefully peeled back the edge of the wrapping paper to discover a shoebox sized box.

"Before you open it, please understand that I am not here in any official capacity but more like in the manner of a curious friend searching for answers." He said like a schoolboy wanting an answer from his teacher to a difficult problem.

Before opening up the wrapped up box I looked at the writing on the wrapping and asked "Who wrote this to you?" almost afraid to ask or know. "It is my own hand writing that you see there but I never sent it to my knowledge or did I? I hope that you two can spread some light on it.

"How can we help you? Neither of us knows what or why you would send yourself something" said Jane, trying to appear as naively innocent as she could.

"Open it and see what there is." came his calm response, so being somewhat curious myself, I gently lifted off the box lid and peered inside.

Inside it I found a mass of papers, photographs what resembled official reports with a cassette tape and a hand written letter in John's own writing addressed to himself.

"Why on earth would anyone send themselves a letter or package?" I asked trying to appear as ignorant on the subject as I could.

On John's urging, Jane went into our kitchen to make us all a pot of tea, while I picked out the small number of photos and sat back on our couch to browse over them. The first picture was a close up of a grave stone with written on it the words `here lays the body of Jane Thompson tragically taken from us on the 11th August 1998 but never forgotten` which had been taken only a few days previously for us. Next was a photograph taken from a short distance away showing an open grave, complete with an open coffin and cordoned off by police crime scene tape with John standing beside it holding up a news paper, showing the date only a matter of days previously.

Jane was sitting beside me trying to look surprised and shocked but not that well asked what this was all about.

"What has it got to do with me?" Jane asked, while swiping at her long, wavy blonde hair from her eyes.

"I think a lot more than you want to tell." John replied. Unexpectedly he handed me an official coroner's report congratulating us on our coming baby, a baby which was not going to be found out about for a few more weeks yet. Not thinking I slipped up and immediately thanked him, not remembering that she had only just conceived but it had not yet been confirmed.

Sounding pleased with himself John said, "So it's all true and has happened just as all this information says, you did die and have come back to life. There must be a reason why, perhaps you have a destiny to fulfil." Pausing to look at our faces he carried on with, "So that explains why when I went to the church earlier and looked around the graveyard there was not a sign of any open grave or tomb stone with Jane's name on it. All this stuff confirms that time has in some way been altered, to bring you back." said John in a mixture of both relief and bewilderment.

Although I think we were all asking ourselves the same question it was Jane in her inquisitive way who said "I don't understand why or how you have all this stuff now because now nothing has happened. I have not died and come back to life. So tell me why you think you know this John and what are you going to do about it?"

Taking a deep breath, he made us unsure about the future when he said "It appears that I am meant to know everything what has happened with you otherwise the contents of this box would not still be here." Pausing and looking directly into our faces he went on to say, "I suspect there is another reason why I have been allowed to know all this, perhaps your experience with death and return to life connects you Jane to something else equally as miraculous." His statement filled our minds with much as we tried to think of why we had been contacted and how John had known what had happened plus did anybody else know.

After about another hour of talking, it was decided that concerning Jane and I, it was best that nobody else could ever know about it, so in our presence, John burnt the evidence of everything that had happened which he had brought in the box with him, Also we decided to keep in touch in case anything new happened. By new I mean ghostly or supernatural and by the December nothing had occurred worthy of our paying attention to so the two of us set about preparing for the festive break not knowing that things were about to happen, things that affect all of our lives including that of Lindsey's.

It was as the chimes from the town's sixteenth century clock tower started to ring in the coming New Year, just like it had done the year before when Jane's ghost had first appeared to me while beside her grave. Only this time it was as Lindsey was raising her glass to toast the future as we entered the year of 1999 again when Jane seemed to suddenly freeze where she was sitting, with her face turning bluer and a completely blank look appeared on her face before her mouth opened to speak; only the voice we heard was that of an older lady with great sadness in it. Lindsey being frightened stopped in mid sentence and her mouth dropped as we heard the woman's voice say, "God used the power of the eclipse to bring Jane back from the dead so please do it again and save the children, and the others," finishing off with "I'm begging you to please help them." Then Jane collapsed into my arms and thankfully for us nobody else where we were had noticed anything. It was only a matter of seconds before she came around again saying, "What happened?" when her eyes opened "are we being called on babe?"

Turning to face me she told me what had just happened to her asking what could we do, to which I suggested telling John and seeing if he could help us to identify the woman whose spirit had just appeared to her. I was not too sure about calling him because of the nature of why, but I think we both knew that if we were being called on to prevent the deaths of many, we would almost certainly be needing his help. For the rest of the night, we managed to dismiss what had just happened as foolish tomfoolery as a result of our drinking, but our talk was filled of questions mostly from Lindsey about what she had seen happen to her best friend and coming back to life with the eclipse because for everyone else including her it was about six months in the future that it was due.

For Jane and myself we were more concerned about discovering who's involved, the where it was happening where ever it was and more importantly when and why.

It must of been about five in the morning that we arrived back home, after swearing Lindsey to secrecy, whilst warning her of the potential dangers to all of us if the wrong people found out any of it. When we reached home I left a message for John on his answering machine asking him to contact us then Jane and I went to bed our minds full of thoughts of what had happened to her earlier.

Come morning we were not surprised when John knocked on our door carrying a note book ready for making notes if needed when we shared with him the news following the previous night. "Mrs Sarah

Donaldson is or was her name, the woman we need to trace who contacted me." relayed Jane as she told of our experience and the plea for help from beyond, that she had received as we and Lindsey drank the New Year in.

"Well I guess I can run a trace on her name and see what I can find out about her, do you have any idea as to when she died or how?" said John, intrigued by what he had just heard.

"All I can say is she's called Sarah Donaldson and I could smell burning fuel and bodies" added Jane. As we spoke I was amazed at how John being a big built man and able to portray such authority and control just sat there on our couch mesmerized by what he was learning. Until we knew about Sarah Donaldson, where she died, how she died and who the children that her spirit wanted us to save were. There was little that we could do other than wait for news from John on his investigation to identify her. Also we couldn't forget the fact that I had a job to go to and for the girls they had their modelling work to keep them busy and for Jane herself she had to put her unborn baby first.

Keeping the task that we had embarked on fresh in my mind at all times I had to carry on as normal with my usual daily routine so I kissed Jane goodbye and set off to my job at a local supermarket. As I walked up the main street past the shoe shop, the opticians, WH Smiths, Peacocks clothes store and a branch of Lloyds bank, I couldn't help but ask myself if what we were doing was intended by God because if successful many souls would not be going to the other side as had already happened during the past year.

"Mike! Wait for me." came Lindsey's voice calling from the window of a bus as it slowed to stop at its stop outside of a newsagents shop. "Are you at home tonight because I have been offered a job posing for some posters advertising an air show at the county show this year."

At that time nobody could have known that the very same air show that Lindsey would be promoting through her modelling work would be the same venue that Jane was asked to save the children at by the spirit of Sarah Donaldson. We carried on walking along together until I had to turn off for my work and she crossed the road and round a bend leading to a crescent where all along the outer edge were offices of the town council and legal firms, while on the inner side was a grassed area with seating for walkers. This was the same area where Jane and I often had sat and talked a lot after her near rape experience before leaving school and finding love with me.

Arriving at my work I was just about to enter when my mobile phone let me know that I had just received a text message, which on checking, was from Jane, informing me that John was going to stop by on his way home after coming off duty that night to let us know what he had found out from his checking on Sarah Donaldson. She also informed me she had started to suffer from morning sickness over half way through her pregnancy. Hearing from him I hoped would let us know who she was and with luck where to look for the coming saving from death of many. With that I found the rest of the day seeming to pass quite quickly and soon I was leaving work and going home again, to prepare for our coming visitors that night.

Walking through the front door I was greeted by Jane throwing her arms around me before leading me into the lounge where John and Lindsey were waiting. "Hi guys what's the news." I asked. "I've been tracing as many Sarah Donaldson's as I can." Was the reply from John to my question "I have found three people so far, one is a ninety-three year old from Scotland, one is an eighteen year old student from London and the other is a fifty-four year old junior school teacher from a place called Hadleigh in the county of Suffolk. From what you have told me so far I suspect that she must be the Sarah Donaldson who we are looking for but for what?" said John in his detective voice. With that, we all sat down around our lounge discussing what we should be doing now until late into the night when something happened to clarify our goal.

During the course of our conversation, John informed us that he soon expected to be busy policing a future protest action by those protesters set against a company that were planning to do some exploratory fracking drilling on the waste ground just outside of the town. "What's fracking?" I asked trying not to appear too stupid in front of the others. "I'm not too sure, but I believe it's about getting gas out of the rock in the ground below us." He replied. "I've heard about that" said Lindsey, continuing with "I saw a news report blaming it for causing small earthquakes somewhere that does not normally get them."

"Whether it does or not we can bet that whoever does it will pay an expert to say it's safe. It'll be the likes of the police to stop the protesters." We all hoped that the company wanting to drill would change its mind and decide not to do anything.

At that time Lindsey talked Jane into going with her when she posed for the air show advertising, in a selection of different pilot uniforms from various countries, past and present. After getting back home again she described the different outfits saying that she should get one because it looked quite sexy followed by one of her winks and naughty smile. I remember thinking that if she did I certainly would not mind.

It was at 11.55pm when all of us started to smell burning fuel and flesh. Raising her hand over her nose Jane managed to say "What on earth is going on here, it smells like burning skin and petrol." And then it happened, something that would devastate and haunt us for the rest of our lives. It was, as I said, 11.55pm when we started to smell burning fuel and flesh and we were wanting to know its source that our attention was drawn to an image of I guess Sarah Donaldson. She said only a few words which were "Remember what you will see and make the right choice." Then a very bright flash of light briefly dazzled all of us and on being able to see again we discovered that we had somehow been placed amongst the massive crowd of spectators watching a display of Ariel manoeuvring by two world war one bi planes entertaining them.

As we watched one of the planes clip the others tail end, causing it to break off sending the plane plummeting toward earth. More than that was the plane was right over a long wooden stand with seating for the onlookers. Amid the screams of horror everyone started clambering to get clear, tripping over each other and pushing in panic to escape from what was about to happen.

As the plane fell I, could see the brave pilot wrestling with the controls trying to steer it clear, with little success. None of the four of us could move, meaning that we were about to be at the centre of the crash. Jane and Lindsey screamed in horror while John and I struggled with our legs trying to move and expecting to die. The pilot was managing to direct the plane clear but it was no use because the plane smashed straight into a parked fuel tanker behind the stand.

The whole sky lit up as the tanker exploded into a huge ball of flame which engulfed the whole length of the stand where the four of us were caught like the over a hundred and fifty other people unable to get clear and were being turned into figures of flame. Although we were unable to move from where we stood, the wave of fire that flowed across the entire stand never touched us enabling us all see what the crowd saw as they were dying. It was John who first noticed that at one end of the stand were a party of junior school aged children with staff on a day excursion from their school.

After we had witnessed the catastrophe, another bright light returned us our lounge where the girls clung onto each other, traumatised by what we had seen, while both John and I fell to the floor, speechless by what we had just seen. "How can something so bad be allowed to happen to so many young children?" I managed to say while still crying at what we had seen.

"Maybe that is why you were contacted Jane, to put right what should never happen by God." said John, who was trying to make some sort of sense out of the whole thing. It didn't take much for us to know what we had to do and the reason why. I doubt that any of us were able to get any sleep that night and we could not dare tell anyone, which meant that we could never get professional help with dealing with it.

CHAPTER 2

By the morning I believe that we all knew what we had to do, but to be honest, I had no idea how we could stop one plane from causing another one to crash unintentionally. Basically we had to prevent the accident to save 138 lives, including 56 children, by stopping the crash from happening. As I made a pot of tea for Jane and I my mind was filled with what we had to do, until everything became unimportant, when Jane came out of our bedroom and told me of her night.

"Someone spoke to me in my sleep last night and now I'm not sure if we should do anything." "Not do anything! With all that we saw last night, what were you told?" I asked in disbelief at what she had just said, knowing that she was the sort of person who would gladly give her life for another who deserved to live. "It was a deep voice and it felt very cold and bad." Pausing she carried on with, "I think it was the devil and it wants their souls, what do we do, Mike?"

After suggesting that we talk with John and Lindsey before we did anything I left her for work as I always did after breakfast.

During the day, John who had been finding out as much as he could about places that can put on air shows, like the one where the crash was due to happen so was somewhat surprised when we told him about Jane's dream message. When I told him he quite angrily said, "I don't understand, just think of the tens of thousands of people that die every year that we don't know in advance about but this time we do know everything that will happen before it does and we can stop it from ever happening. To me this one thing gives my life a sense of purpose. You can choose to do nothing because of a message in a dream, but I am going to do anything to save them kids."

Obviously he was quite right in what he said making me feal a little petty.

He was right of course but all the same we were concerned as to what would happen if we helped. It was Jane who decided that we had to help, after she had been returned to life after she was killed a year before the full eclipse which is due to happen again this year. "Thank you John you just helped us understand what is at stake if we do nothing, so tell us what you have found out so far."

"The show is due to be held on the site of a world war one airfield in Kent and tomorrow I should know the names of the pilots involved. What we need to know is which pilot is the one who crashed and which one caused it because maybe we can stop him from flying." Before leaving our place John enquired about where Lindsey was that day and what would she be doing to help us. "She flew out of Heathrow this morning for a modelling assignment in the Caribbean and should be gone about a week."

"Lucky cow getting paid to work in the Sun and leave us with the cold and wet. I bet she comes back with a good tan on her" proclaimed John as he was leaving. Now we had committed ourselves to the task ahead, we called it a night and were preparing ourselves to go to bed and feeling like we were doing the right thing, not knowing that again Jane would get another message, this time while I was there, by means of an image in our wall mirror.

The image in the mirror resembled a silhouetted figure of a human saying "If you stop it happening, I will take your souls for mine. Just so you know that I will your friend will die very soon." Just as it finished speaking its eyes lit up, in a bright piercing red glow, which told us that an evil spirit had plans to steal many souls. Straight away Jane got on her mobile phone and rang Lindsey

After what felt like hours, from the other end of the phone came the very upset voice of Lindsey saying,

"I should have stayed at home sis. There are so many dead and I was meant to be on the same bus that has crashed."

There had been a very traumatic crash killing everyone who was travelling on a bus where Lindsey was. As Jane consoled Lindsey I went over and switched on the TV putting on a 24hour news channel to see if there was any news, there was. It soon transpired that a bus which had been hired to transport guests to the Caribbean Paradise Hotel where Lindsey was booked in to stay during her work had ran off the road and over a cliff into a steep sided ravine killing all of the 43 passengers on board and the driver.

After ending her call Jane turned her head toward me and said, wiping the tears from her eyes, "All those people have been killed because we are trying to stop the plane accident. It's our fault it has happened and we almost lost my best friend as well. Maybe we shouldn't carry on with this." "We have to finish this; it's why you were contacted in the first place." "What if anyone else dies because of what we are doing? I wish I knew why out of all the deaths during the time after my return these people need to be saved?" Thinking for a moment for the right thing to say I ended with, "Try to think of it as a coincidence it happening then and the evil one took credit for it to scare us into doing what he wants us to do, and there must be a reason for saving them." We never told Lindsey or John what happened that night before the bus crash or I feel that they might think twice about helping us.

It was the second week of February and we were each making our own arrangements to spend our night at a Valentine's party or dance. Jane and I had tickets to go to my works staff do, John unfortunately was working and Lindsey was due to join in a party from her employers, but all was about to become a living hell for us.

We were just leaving home when the light in our lounge switched on suddenly without the switch being touched "What the heck has happened." said Jane dumfounded by what had just happened, so I turned around and walked back into our lounge to check. The first thing that I noticed on entering our lounge was our TV which had turned on and then I saw our mirror, with a not right reflection in it.

"Jane! I called out, I think we are about to get a visitation from beyond. I could hear the sound of her coming back into our place as I watched a shear black shadow form in the centre of the screen with a pair of piercing red eyes appear. It didn't take much time for us to know where the reflection had come from, an evil one. Trying to look as calm and relaxed as she could Jane asked, "What do you want now, you evil piece of shit." I can tell that Jane was putting on an act because I was as frightened as she was.

"You ignored my warning before, now you can watch as I take your friends soul. With that the image in our mirror faded and another one formed. This one was one of the bedrooms where Lindsey was staying and we could see her sitting at her vanity table brushing her shoulder length straight hair before going to work. We could plainly see that whatever function she was planning to attend must be a big one by the expensive looking dress that she was laid out on her bed ready to put on.

Right there in our wall mirror we could see as Lindsey suddenly dropped her hair brush and lifted her hands against her cheeks seeming to scream. Although we couldn't see her face we could see its reflection in her vanity mirror and it looked so horrific when we saw her face literally melting away from her skull with her blood squirting in all ways as her eyeballs fall onto the floor before her body burst into flames where she stood. What we saw was so bad that Jane fainted into a heap on the floor and I rushed into our bathroom to be sick.

We had both seen that Hollywood special effects could mimic what we had seen that night but to actually see it happen for real was bad enough to drive some mad or even suicidal. For me personally I was reminded of how while Jane's spirit was in limbo between life and death it had used Lindsey's body to make love with me and how I had grown an extent of romantic love for her in the process. Now we had both just witnessed the deadly power of the evil one as she was dying in the most horrific way so far away from her home.

Jane had spent the night in tears over the murder of our friend and I had just sat staring at a bare wall trying to make sense out of what had happened. "Do you think that we should call John and tell him what happened last night because I am sure that he will find out at some point today?" I asked before picking up the phone to call him. I needn't have asked because before I could call our phone rang and it was him. "Have you seen the news today?" "I guess it's about Lindsey's murder last night."

"How do you know that?" he asked "I'll explain later." was my reply to him. After saying he was on his way over I called Jane informing her of our coming guest.

"How is she?" was the first thing that John asked when he arrived and then she walked out of our bedroom her face all puffy after crying so much at her loss. "We saw it all taking place John. She was killed by that bastard evil one as punishment for us not giving up on saving all those people."

There was a silence for a while before John continued with, "On the TV news the Authorities say that they think she was scarified as part of some sort of Satanist ritual but they have nothing to go on so far to find the guilty. Her remains will be flown back home during the next few days. I'll let you know where and when her funeral is when I can so you can go to show your respect." That evening the two of us spoke a lot about whether or not to continue with our task of saving those killed by the biplane crash or leave it to prevent any more deaths by the evil one. By the morning we had decided that to quit was not what Lindsey would have done so carrying on would be a way of honouring her memory.

A week later on the fifth day of March we received a call from John informing us of the funeral of our friend so we made the necessary arrangements to be there to pay homage to her memory. We stood there heads bowed in a certain amount of guilt because she had only died because of our determination to prevent the deaths of so many innocents who had already died in the pre eclipse time."I wish I knew that we are doing the right thing." commented Jane wiping another tear from her eye while thinking of her best friend. "You are" came a comforting voice in both of our heads continuing with "You must save them because the child of the grand child of one of them is destined to save all life on earth from destruction by those that allow their greed for profit and power overrule everything that I intended for humanity. Do this and your friend will be returned."

If we succeed in preventing the deaths Lindsey will be brought to life again. Both of us were very happy and relieved at what we had been told, but we could not see anyone except the mourners, even so we knew who was talking to us. Now we knew the importance of what we were doing and we felt justified in our actions. Looking around at the other mourners I saw apart from her family and relatives, several of our school class mates, her agent from her work, a local photographer who she had modelled for and a newspaper journalist covering the funeral for a national paper.

When we got home I cut out from a newspaper a tribute to Lindsey that had been printed along with a photograph of her as a reminder of how much she meant to all of us before placing it in a frame which I found unused in a box of bits and pieces in the bottom of a kitchen cupboard, before fixing it to the lounge wall to the side of our TV.

The next day I told John about our experience at the funeral which made him as happy as we were, more so because we had decided to carry on and finish what we had started but because of what happened to Lindsey he more or less insisted that from then on Jane should not be involved in any way. Obviously she was not happy about his suggestion until he pointed out the fact that she was going to be a mother soon and our baby was too important.

"You do not want the same thing as happened to Lindsey to happen to your baby or you." he said, which had me contented by his concern for Jane and our unborn baby. I suggested that Jane visited her mother for a little time while John and I checked out a new night club on the edge of town that was beginning to get visited by many under aged children and was attracting unsavoury older men. This was a concern to the police but being monitored by them already along with the club owners. Under this excuse the two of us were able to make plans for how on earth to stop a plane from crashing and killing so many without Jane becoming involved or even knowing what we were doing.

Sitting in a local Mc Donald's take away with a cup of tea John took out his note book and started flicking through the pages until he found the page that he wanted. "I've found out as much as I can about the pilots involved. One and I believe the one who died was a retired RAF pilot is called James Morris with over 30 years of service to the crown. The other one is a rich want to be amateur that has used with his own money to learn to fly himself. He can fly but does not have the necessary skill to perform the split second manoeuvres being planned." "So what we need to do is find a way to stop their display from being used and prevent what we all saw from happening." I replied to his information. Bearing that in mind, we knew what was going to happen, we had to come up with an idea of how to stop the collision with the inevitable outcome.

Getting home again my mind was filled with ways to stop the crash without going against the law or harming either pilot to stop them flying. I wanted so much to talk with Jane and hear her thoughts on what to do but we had to keep her from knowing our plans and preventing them from being found out by the evil one.

After having something to eat the two of us settled down on our couch so that Jane could tell me about her day. "Hey guess what, I've been asked to model some maternity clothes by a store." "That's great sweetheart, you can get paid for having a bump." I replied jokingly. "Oh I've got an appointment at the hospital for a scan tomorrow afternoon and we need to decide if we want to know the sex of our baby in advance of the birth. I'd rather not know in advance." I agreed with her as long as it was ok. We talked some more before at 11.55pm the smell of burning fuel and flesh filled our nostrils and an image of Sarah Donaldson followed by one of a fuel tanker. Come morning I somehow knew that Jane had received a message or instruction in her sleep which was shown when she said. "Think of preventing the explosion instead of the crash it may be easier. You might have to let a pilot die to save the others."

Three days later on the Friday night John came around to discuss what I had decided on doing as we were getting closer to the air show date. "Jane has been told in a dream that we should forget the planes and concentrate on the tanker, and another thing is our baby's due date is the twenty ninth of May only a couple of days before the air show."

The next day I accompanied Jane to the hospital situated in the next town for her scan to check on the development of our coming baby. I will never forget the feeling of pride with my darling Jane and I too on hearing the heart beat. When the consultant carrying out the scan said that it looked healthy and with nothing to be concerned over we were both over the moon. "Why don't we go and visit your parents and let them that their grand-child is going to be ok." I said trying to curtain the joyful feelings inside under control while at the same time being a certain amount scared at the threat of death made by the evil one against my beautiful loving fiancée before killing our dear friend Lindsey.

Whilst we appeared to be living a usual life with me going to my work and Jane doing her modelling maternity clothes for a national clothing chain and whilst having her belly get larger with our child growing inside of her, John was busy gathering all the necessary information that would help us when it came time to act, like obtaining access to the cab of the tanker and where to find a spare key to start the engine in order to move it. As he said it felt as if we were planning some sort of criminal enterprise and jokingly suggested arresting himself which did make us laugh knowing that doing so would save lives and would secure all of our futures.

On the day a few days before the end of May, John who having borrowed a police car under the pretence of escorting the school children's coach to the show through the heavy traffic, which was expected by the organisers. After collecting me on route we met the coach and drove to the show arriving in enough time for the show which was just starting with a display by the red arrows. At home, what we didn't know was that Jane was getting admitted to the maternity hospital as she had gone into labour a few days past her due date thanks to Lindsey who had agreed to be with her whilst I was not at home for her.

When the time finally arrived for action we knew that in a matter of minutes a plane was going to crash killing so many innocent people, but we had made our own plans to stop it from happening. John and I found our way to a suitable place to watch events unwind away from the spectators stand just in case we failed.

"I'm going to check out a few things." said John standing up and casually walking around behind the stand toward the fuel tanker. Wearing his officer's identification badge as a way of not being thought of as a criminal or as though he did not belong there, he tried the driver's side door and found it unlocked. In the air way up above us came the sound of the two bi-planes coming in to start their display so John carefully opened the tankers door and climbed up into the cab. After checking it he found a spare ignition key tucked behind the sun blind and started the engine.

Suddenly there was a cracking sound from above accompanied by screams from the crowd as one plane caught the others tail, ripping it off and making it start to fall uncontrollably toward the earth along with the falling tail end of one of the planes. That was the signal John needed and he started the tankers engine driving it about fifty meters forward away from where we knew the plane would hit. As I plainly observed, rather than bailing out and falling safely with a parachute, the retired RAF pilot James Morris bravely stayed in the plane fighting with its controls trying to direct it away from the crowd. As the falling plane fell, it briefly disappeared from sight behind the crowds stand and then there was a loud thud as it hit. But this time there was no massive explosion and wave of fire killing everyone.

As the emergency crews rushed to the crash I saw a TV news reporter standing in front of the camera telling the viewers about what she had just witnessed, and the sudden surprise when out of the wreckage clambered the pilot without as much as a single scratch on him. After taking the time to bow to the onlookers James Morris strolled over to the reporter to give an interview starting with a question,

"Where is that man who just moved the tanker out of the way? He has just saved many lives through his act." But nobody could say who it was as no-one was meant to be in it or move it. "How did you avoid being hurt?" asked the reporter but his reply would have people asking questions for a long time to come.

He said, "I have no idea what happened to me up there but I swear that just before I hit the tanker, a massive hand appeared from out of nowhere and surrounded me until after I hit, keeping me safe, it was a miracle like the person who moved the tanker." "Does anyone know who it was because whoever it is was is not a worker from here? It's like they knew what was going to happen in advance." said the chief of the ground staff who had just arrived on the scene.

With that over, John and I made our way back to his car and departed the air field heading for home both of us feeling contented with our actions on that day. As he drove his car, John expressed how he wished he knew what, by saving the unknown child whose descendent would save the world, would have happened if we hadn't done anything. We had just joined the M5 motorway heading for Exeter when my mobile phone started ringing and on answering it I received even more good news. "Mike my darling, I am at the hospital, we've had a baby girl born at exactly seventeen minutes past one pm. I will be discharged in about two hours after all the necessary checks are done with her." "We should be close enough to pick her up if you want Mike." offered John which I excitedly accepted knowing that during the time taken to save any lives I had just become a father to a little girl. As we drove back John switched on the car radio to listen to some music catching an interview with the other pilot from the show claiming that he was not going to fly anymore because of what had and would almost certainly of happened because of his error at the show.

As we drove along the motorway we talked a lot about ourselves and our families, "I've been wondering about your sir name John, does it come from a different country because it sounds like it is?" I asked inquisitively. "It's from India, my family moved here about two hundred years ago.

Before collecting Jane from the maternity ward at the hospital, John wanted to stop off at his home so that he could change his clothes for his usual off duty ones which were jeans and sweat shirt. Whilst he did what he wanted to do I stayed in his police car and listened to the radio talking a lot about the incident at the air show and playing the recorded interview with the pilot who would now be dead, if not for the mysterious man that moved a fuel tanker in time to avoid a devastating explosion that could have killed dozens of people and the unexplainable feeling of being held as the plane crashed, protecting him from harm. When he returned I could sense a feeling of success in him as John got back into the car casually pulling out, heading for the hospital and Jane.

CHAPTER 3

After we had stopped to pick up a bouquet of flowers to give to Jane for when we collected her from the maternity hospital where she had been admitted earlier that day to give birth, we parked in the necessary space to collect her and then returned to our home, only to get another surprise. It was as we entered our front door with Jane walking a little unsteadily after giving birth, John carrying her case and I holding our baby, that Jane instantly noticed that the tribute to Lindsey which we had kept after her funeral had disappeared from where we had placed it on our lounge wall next to a framed photograph of the two of them taken on their last day of school.

"Have you taken down Lindsey's tribute darling?" asked Jane.

I replied, "No babe, I haven't touched it." Then John being aware of past happenings suggested, "Maybe one of you should check out her grave or perhaps give her a call on her mobile."

"That's a good idea; I'll try her number once we get mummy and baby sorted out. Oh, we had better decide on a name for her as well." I said. "After all that has happened to all of us this last year or so I think that we should call her Faith because we have had to have it, to do what has been required of us." Jane said in reply to me.

Looking down at our baby Faith she smiled seeming to approve of Jane's choice of name for her. With that decided on, I suggested the two of us take both sets of parents out for a meal to give them firstly Faith's name and secondly ask for their blessing to get married, but for now Jane wanted and needed to try and contact Lindsey.

We needn't have done anything about checking up on Lindsey as Jane's ringing mobile soon revealed. "I'm going to come and see you tomorrow because I need to pass on a message to you, Mike and if possible, John as well. I need to know what has happened to me, all I remember is sitting at the makeup mirror in my hotel room and then my face felt like it was on fire, then I was in a room surrounded by many others being led out one of two doors one by one. Was I dead again sis?" she said inquisitively before passing on her congratulations over her giving birth.

"I'll leave it to Mike to explain everything to you tomorrow Lin's, he knows what has happened and why. I'm just so happy that you have come back to us." said Jane obviously overjoyed with knowing that her best friend had again escaped an early death. But first we had to feed and change Faith who was sleeping in her mothers` arms while she talked on the phone.

Another thing that John wanted to do was to telephone the junior school and enquire as to the reaction to the air show which came back with nothing but praise, and after seeing the pilot's interview on the t v thanks for the unknown person who had moved the tanker saving their lives.

Once arrangements had been made ahead of the following day May 29 1999 John said his goodbye's and left Jane and I for the rest of the day enabling us to do what all new parents do for our daughter. We also telephoned both sets of new grandparents to give them the good news of one more to add to our family trees and to arrange us all going out for an evening meal, trusting Lindsey and John's wife Carol to look after Faith for a few hours on the Saturday night.

At a little after two pm the following day Lindsey arrived and with tears of joy in her eyes Jane threw her arms around her friends neck hugging her as if she were a family member who had been away for many years. Once they had finished hugging Jane took her friend by the hand and led her into our lounge saying, "Come and meet Faith. Mike is holding her now so you can meet and hold our baby." Continuing with, "Will you be her God mother." I was just about to fill her in on everything when a knock at our door let us know that John had arrived so I temporarily, held talking to Linsey in order to answer it.

"Lindsey is alive and well again after what you did at the show my friend. She is here now." I said on opening the door, as if I had just spoken about his daughter or winning the lottery. On seeing him as we re-entered our lounge, Lindsey threw her arms around his neck and thanked him for saving her life, as well as all of the children that were as dead as she had been before the plane crash which was avoided by his action in moving the tanker.

With all 'welcome backs' and 'thank you's' said, I made us all a pot of tea and Jane saw to Faiths needs before sitting down to listen to the message that Lindsey had been told to pass on and John also had something to tell us, from a dream he had the night before. Having seen him arrive unshaven and not at ease with himself or something else I enquired as to what was playing on his mind to which he said, "Ok I'll tell you and then you may feel as badly as I did over it"

Feeling his rough chin he said, "Remember how I said about knowing what would happen if we hadn't saved the child who has the destiny that we were told of. Well, I saw it and I cried for the things that humans greed for money and power will do to this planet and our home if this child fails in its foretold destiny."

"Well come on then, tell us what you saw" said Jane inquisitively. Continuing with his description John relayed his dream to us sniffing back a tear at what he had seen.

"I saw the Amazon rain forest burning so the ground could be built and grown on without a slightest thought or consideration being given to the effect on the world's climate, the wild life and environment or the lives of the native peoples that live there, and the ice caps melted causing many places to flood including London and a lot of New York "Taking a breath before carrying on with, "Another thing I saw was the way that the earth's crust was breaking up due to the countless companies mining for coal and minerals and drilling for oil. The mines and wells are starting to cave in making the surface sink. That is damaging the natural earth's surface causing more earthquakes and volcanic eruptions, killing millions on every continent. It has already started in small ways but it's being denied and the reason for it covered up by the big international companies and corrupt politicians who are getting rich from it".

He went on." At one point I saw an entire town in the United States sink into the ground as a new volcano erupted in the crater. It must have killed over a million people. Another thing I saw was an earthquake splitting California off from the rest of America; only it sank into the sea, killing countless people. That was because open casting had weakened the San Andria's fault, causing massive earthquakes. It's not too late yet and can be prevented as long as the child with the destiny to do so does."

Pausing for a breath before he continued with his tale he brushed his hand across his brow. "How many innocent people would have to die because of business greed for profit? The worse thing that I saw is what would happen here is on the ground next to the approach road into our town. I saw that a fracking operation had caused a small earthquake, leading to the earth splitting open and leaving a huge trench the entire length of the high street, bursting the gas and water mains and the buildings on either side of it to start falling into the trench on top of the traffic that had already fallen. I also saw one school bus covered by the front of the newsagents before any children could get out and clear of it. Thankfully I'll be long dead and buried before it could happen but it scares the hell out of me the level of destruction that we could cause and the amount of animals and plants that would become extinct because of us".

"What sort of world are we leaving to our descendants?" commented Jane looking either way to check our response's at what we had just heard. Now we all had the knowledge of what we all had to do during the years ahead, if we want our planet to survive as God intended it for us. Having seen a sneak preview of what future generation might have to face if nothing changes, I think we all felt a certain anger and sense of betrayal of every living thing on the planet, by those who worship profit and power above life and the beautiful planet on which we all live and depend on. I had never realised that if we continued treating the earth so badly we would not have anywhere else to go and live.

Realising that our baby Faith's own grand children would be affected by the possible horrific future I was so grateful that John had saved the child with the destiny to save us but at the same time felt sorry for the ones that would be killed needlessly beforehand. We will never be able to watch a natural disaster movie again without remembering what John told us that day with a tear in our eye. It strikes me as unbelievable the way that I had changed from being a non believer only two years before, to someone who does not practise any religion but does not have the slightest doubt that God does exist and is watching over us at all times whoever and wherever we are.

Next it was Lindsey's turn to share what she had to say, so turning her gaze to Jane she started to speak. "When I was in the big room that felt like it was a waiting room before I was returned to life, I was talking to a man there who said that he was called Peter Maclean and had been murdered but is being blamed for stealing twelve million pounds from the bank where he worked and now his wife and children are suffering from threats and lies from others including his bosses and the national press. Can you find his body because a post-mortem will prove that he was murdered and was innocent so that his family can have closure over his death? He was quite a good looker as well."

Going on, she enquired, "I suppose it's a silly question, John, but do you have any idea about the man I just told you about?"

"I may be wrong but it sounds like the case of the bank worker who stole a fortune and disappeared, we thought he had done a runner overseas. The police here, the euro police and even Interpol are investigating." was his reply to her.

"It looks like you are all wrong." I added getting intrigued by what we had just heard and wondering what we were hoped could do about it. The sound of Faith crying brought our get together to an abrupt end so John gave Lindsey a lift home before he went to work, I think with what we now knew fresh in his mind.

On the Saturday night Jane and I met both sets of parents, proudly showing off the dozen or so photographs taken of mother and baby during the short while since coming home. Jane's parents Russell and Debra and mine David and Marie were all mesmerised as they looked closely at every picture of their granddaughter. The most exuberant moment came when holding her hand in mine I knelt down on one knee and asked Jane to marry me which was unanimously welcomed and was answered by everyone with a "yes" and by my love with, "I will marry you" finishing off with a kiss.

During the following days until July tenth there was no news from John, Lindsey had travelled to Greece working, I was busy at work and Jane was enjoying being a new mother but that changed for us at 11.55pm when just like our previous experiences an image formed in our wall mirror showing a tied and gagged man being shot execution style in the back of the head followed by the words, "This is how I was killed on a farm in Suffolk close to a train track. There were six of them involved. Tell my family that I was not bad and I did not desert them like the press said I did." He also told us the date and time of it happening which would be helpful for us and then the image disappeared back to normal. We were both shocked by what we had just seen and felt very sorry for the affect that it must have had on the poor man's family.

It was the evening of the twelfth that we spoke to John again telling him about what we had seen in our mirror and after a short moment he said. "We know how Jane was able to come back and how we stopped the deaths at the air-show from happening I wonder if we can in some way prevent his murder and maybe prevent the crime from happening before the eclipse next month. Could a miracle happen again or will we have to settle for only a closure for his family?"

Speaking with John he found out that the crime in question was carried out on the day of the eclipse in 1999 time itself and the crime had been planned to coincide with it, the idea being to use the brief darkness during the eclipse to steal the money.

Rubbing her chin in thought Jane posed the question, "If we know what is going to happen and when can we make an anonymous call or even set a trap and catch the criminals in the act." "I'm way ahead of you young lady and I'll deal with it tomorrow." answered John in his official policeman's voice quite pleased at her way of thinking. When Lindsey called the next day I had the pleasure of informing her of what was being set in motion by John and when we might be hearing about it on the news which pleased her immensely plus we would not need to do anything.

The next day the day of the eclipse Jane and I found that just like the previous time we were unable to witness natures gift of an eclipse because there was thick cloud coverage so we settled for sitting in front of the TV watching the reports from other areas and more importantly watching the news for anything about what John and his fellow officers were going to do regarding the big robbery. It wasn't until the national and international news came on the BBC channel at six pm that we heard the saddening news that during a police operation to capture a gang of robbers an officer had been shot while rescuing and the freeing of bank employee Peter Maclean.

Luckily he had not been seriously injured but was taken to hospital for treatment. Obviously, Jane had to call Lindsey and tell her what had just happened for which she thanked her asking us to deliver a bouquet of flowers to his bedside from her while he convalesced. In order to keep our knowledge of what was going down and how John claimed that he had heard it being planned by a couple of people that he was unable to see in a public bar.

So all in all during the space of two years we had witnessed the same eclipse twice, helped save over a hundred people from death after a plane crash, stopped a robbery and murder, Lindsey had almost died of cancer and been killed by an evil spirit before returning to life and most importantly, Jane had been returned to life after her being killed in an accident. With all of us we had discovered that sometimes God will use people to help others to do the right thing while in a way testing our own faith and trust in him and ourselves.

CHAPTER 4

By the first of September 1999 our lives had not only been given the 12 months between Jane's tragic death in an accident and an eclipse which brought her back to life and me, to live again and be blessed with the birth of our daughter Faith. Along with Jane's best friend Lindsey and our new good friend police detective John Ammet plus with the will of God we had prevented the deaths of over a hundred people including many young children after a plane accident at a show thanks to John's courageous action and saving the life of one child who's descendant was destined to save the planet from mankind's own actions and selfish greed. But all that was before the repeated eclipse.

"Now that everything has been done and we are all ok, can we go ahead and arrange our wedding my love?" asked Jane peering very seductively at me from our bed. "Yes of course sweetheart, let's do it quickly before Faith is christened." I replied. Reaching over to her right side to her bedside cupboard she picked up a notepad and pen to begin writing a list of things which we had to do before saying I do to each other, but the sound of our daughter needing her mummy or daddy to take care of her needs soon had us putting our plans on hold to get up and dressed. While Jane worked on her list of necessary things to do I took on the role of taking care of Faith by washing and dressing her before sitting down hand feeding her.

Joining us in the lounge Jane read out her list starting with asking John to be my best man and Faith's Godfather when we had her christened as well as Lindsey, we had to book some time off of work for our wedding and honeymoon, and of course the wedding itself, all jobs that we would be doing together except for the wedding dress that Lindsey would certainly be involved in. Everything felt almost like a fairytale for me but soon enough something happened to scupper our plans causing us both great anguish and worry.

It was on the night of the third Friday of the month that as we were about to turn off the lounge light before going to bed that we both felt a sudden chill pass through our bodies which we hadn't felt since our experiences during the previous year. Automatically we directed our eyes in the direction of the wall mirror where we had seen several dead spirits before including Jane's before her return to life.

We could have been knocked down by feather when the image forming before us was that of one of Jane's school friends called Penny Whitaker. "Oh Penny! What has happened to you?" she murmured seeing a good friend from school was now no more. Unlike the previous times neither of us experienced a movement to the scene of her demise showing us nothing that could help us to understand the circumstances surrounding what had happened to her at such a young age. "It was Wayne Brummet Jane he killed me because I was your friend and he wants revenge after you got him sent to that young offenders place for trying to rape you. You and Mike are both in danger now. You got to stop him Jane." Wayne was the lad who I stopped from raping Jane before we fell in love and now had targeted her friend in his twisted sense of revenge on route to getting us.

That night we had to do a lot of serious thinking about what we were now facing. "Will we ever get a normal life without having to deal with others problems?" asked Jane as she lifted Faith up out of her cradle to cuddle like a child with their favourite dolly. Putting on as brave a face as I could under the circumstances I placed my arm around her waist and said, "Try not to let Wayne bother you my love, I'll go and have a talk with John and see what can be done about him." and then I placed Faith back down into her cradle before leading Jane over to our bed to hopefully sleep which she decided not to do as it was still only the morning.

After we had dressed, washed and eaten that morning I advised Jane to keep our door and windows shut and locked until I returned home because I had decided to visit John and tell him all about the night before. "Ok darling. When you see him why not tell him that we want him to be your best man and be Faith's Godfather." She called out as I walked out onto the road that led into the town.

My heart started to thump faster as I walked when I noticed the reflection of a slow moving car with blacked out windows tailing me. As I speeded up my walking rate the car suddenly increased its speed purposely coming straight at me before swerving not to hit me. Frightened out of my wits aware of Penny's message I turned around and ran as fast as I could back home again scared for my love and our daughter.

When I rounded the last bend in the road back into the one where we lived I was greeted by the sight of the same car that had just swerved at me driving off from opposite our home making me even more concerned about Jane and Faith. Hurriedly rushing in through our front door I called out to Jane "Jane! Jane!, are you both alright, has he got in to you?" "What are you going on about babe? We're both ok, why?" she answered telling me that Wayne had not managed to get into them which eased my worry temporarily, but made me determined not to leave them alone without me to protect them from any threat.

As I relayed to her what had just happened to me and what I had seen in the road outside she was obviously very disturbed saying, "We need to tell the police babe and let them get the bastard before anyone else is attacked or killed by him. Something seriously bad must have happened to him while locked up to turn him so bad." With that she had to call her best friend Lindsey and tell her all about what had happened during the last twenty four hours making her very angry at Wayne and telling us that she was coming around to see us when she returned to the UK after finishing her current modelling job in Europe. "I can't feel sorry for him honey because he has killed Penny our friend." I said angrily afraid in response to her.

"I think that I should get on the phone and check up on her and find out what I can about for death." With that Jane went into our bedroom to get her address book, soon returning and calling the first of many people she knew to find out as much as she could. As we sat on our couch trying to reassure each other all of our uncertainty over what to do became clear to us when, a bullet came smashing through our lounge window crazing my arm before embedding itself into our wall.

Scared out of our wits I decided to firstly call John, briefly forgetting that after his shooting he would not be working but would almost certainly be at home with his wife and children. It was fortunate that I did because he straight away instructed me to keep all possible entrances to our flat locked and not too go out until he or fellow police officer's came to us. One hearing the shot and Janes scream one of our neighbours a retired nurse took us into her flat and dressed my bleeding arm as best she could with what she had handy while we waited for help to come.

It was only about five minutes later that from the road outside we could hear the sound of several police car sirens screeching to a halt outside and car doors being slammed shut. With his left arm up in a sling John called for an ambulance for me as he instructed his fellow officer's what to do while he came in and talked to us about Penny and Wayne after which he called his superiors to fill them in and get a search started for both of them. When the ambulance arrived I refused to go with them and leave Jane and Faith alone which John accepted on seeing my wound was not serious. It was not that long before the media vans started pulling up outside and the occupants of the other flats in the same building as us were escorted out to safety by armed officers through the rain to a place of safety.

By the morning the entire street had been cordoned off and a national man hunt had begun for Wayne after the body of penny had been found in the flat that she rented closer to the college where she had been studying to be a teacher of junior school aged children.

After three days of effort by the authorities with no luck a piece of good news came up by tracing his mobile phone use and signal to within ten miles of our location. Because the forensics people had discovered Penny's diary had mentioned that he intended to shoot us both and burn our bodies to get his revenge on us as well as he had shot penny through the head.

This time the news about Penny hit Jane very hard because there was no way that anyone could bring her back to life again. That did bother us both because if we hadn't talked in court he would almost certainly of avoided his incarceration after trying to rape her. What hurt Jane more was hearing that her friend had been raped and strangled by Wayne before shooting her which might have happened to her if not for my action preventing their earlier encounter at the youth club whilst at school? For me personally that was enough to justify my past action in interfering when something not right was happening to an innocent person.

It was only a matter hours after a crime watch report on the TV before Wayne was spotted by a member of the public sitting in his car outside of the store where I worked.

Because of the number of potential innocent victims if fire arms were used in such a public place the order was given to the army trained police sniper to shoot him to kill if he made any attempt to resist arrest.

After trying to box him in with their squad cars in order to prevent his escape an officer ordered him to surrender. Unfortunately Wayne raised a shot gun and fired in the direction of the police which triggering the single fatal shot by the police marksman killing him outright where he stood causing a sudden panic amongst the unaware public who had been busy with their own shopping but were now screaming in terror and rushing away from the scene for safty. Receiving the news of what had just happened and the realisation that we were no longer at risk of harm or even death from Wayne was understandably welcomed by us all, more so by Jane who straight away threw her arms around me kissing me ever so passionately.

With that finally over our own sleepy, small town was able to give a Hugh sigh of relief as everyone's lives were able to return to normal. Something that under normal circumstances would be welcomed by most, but for us after our talking with John unnerved us both. He informed us that although Wayne was now dead he had been able to make questionable friends while being punished for his attack on Jane and he could easily afford the cost of hiring another to be his bidding if wanted. With that he added that he had been looking into Wayne's finances and found out that only a week earlier he had paid out the sum of £10000 to an unknown party for an unknown reason.

As for us we were able to get on with our own lives such as the organising of our wedding starting with asking John to be my best man and taking on the role of Godfather to Faith. Jane had already asked Lindsey to be a Godmother and the next time that she saw her she intended to ask her to also act as chief bridesmaid. After speaking with the vicar of the very same church where Jane had been buried after her death, following an accident which now hadn't happened after the magic of the eclipse had brought her back to life, we booked our wedding to coincide with her grandparents wedding anniversary.

On the eighteenth day of March 2000 Jane dressed in her specially designed white wedding dress was walked by her proud father up the isle to where I was stood waiting with John by my side as best man to make our vows to each other before our guests and more impotently before God.

CHAPTER 5

It was as we were drinking our morning cup of tea whilst listening to the radio that the broadcast was interrupted with the news that a terrorist bomb had killed over a hundred innocent people at a public event in a European country with more than one hundred injured. Those responsible claimed that they were going to attack anywhere that did not follow their belief which was not most of the world. Governments and leaders all over world were united in their condemnation of this unforgivable act.

Placing our cups down Jane said "I wish that we could turn back the time and stop the evil bastards from ever doing what they have done." "Even saving one of the victims would be a small victory over the evil that is poisoning the minds and hearts of terrorist leaders. But for now let's try to put this out of our heads and go into town and do some shopping." It did not take much time for Jane to get herself and Faith ready to go and soon we were on our way.

Arriving at the town's main street I noticed a marked increase of police officers being seen by the public reassuring them that the threats made earlier by the terrorists had been noticed and were being taken seriously by the government. "Good morning you two and young Faith, how are you today came the sound of our friend John's voice." With the sparkle of happy motherhood on her face Jane replied with, "We're great thank you, but why is there more police out today. Is it because of what was on the news this morning? Do we need to be worried about it happening on the continent?" Cautiously John lowered his voice before informing us of his concerns. "You have heard nothing from me but unofficially higher up are very worried that we are going to be hit soon by the terrorists and can't stop them because all the suspected groups have denied any involvement in it plus a couple terror groups have offered any information they get. I suspect that even they are a bit scared that they will be blamed and attacked for whoever is responsible." He also told me that he was still aware of the potential threat to us paid for by Wayne Brummet before his death. We soon made our goodbyes and carried on with our shopping watching anything unusual around us unexpectedly sharing John's concerns.

We carried on with our shopping unaware of the solitary person who had been tailing us ever since leaving our home that morning. Walking back out of the clothing store were we had just been to buy Faith a new dress because she had grown out of her old one there was a bright flash followed by the sound of a gunshot and I slumped forward landing face down on the ground, I had been shot. A moment later I could see my own dead body just laid there with fresh blood coming out of my belly. Two young men who were nearby without the slightest hesitation threw themselves at the shooter knocking his gun from his hand and bringing him down. Jane who had screamed out in horror rushed forward to me as the general public who were there either stood stunned by what had just happened before them or gathered around to help in any way that they could.

As I watched my own now dead body a brilliant bright light appeared ahead of me and I could make out the figure of my deceased grandmother ready to welcome me to the afterlife but as I reached her everything changed. Gone was my grandmother and light and in its place stood a tall saintly looking man with his hand held up to stop me. "It is not your time yet, you still have a task to do, so return to your body and life and wait for your task that I have chosen you for." With that he vanished and I felt myself drawn back down into my body. The blood that was running out of my belly suddenly started flowing back into me and the bullet that had killed me just popped back out of me falling onto the ground in plain view of everybody there to their astonishment. I was still unconscious during this and Jane who was holding me so tightly and kissing my face still not aware that

I was now not dead had to be helped by a lady who taken a hold of Faith's buggy helped her to regain her composure.

It was only a few minutes before an ambulance escorted by two police cars arrived to take over. Everybody were so thankful to the two courageous young men that had disarmed the shooter and held him down until the police could arrest him. Taking with them an ak47 weapon gun and taping off the scene for the forensics experts to do their work.

As for me the paramedics where just about to ask why I was apparently not dead or even injured despite the fresh blood stains on my shirt with a fresh bullet hole that had appeared in it but from out of nowhere John right on schedule turned up instructing them to take me to the hospital and wait for him to get there which they did as I was still unconscious.

While this was going on John firstly spoke with a hysterical Jane at seeing her new husband murdered before her advised her to go to me at the hospital, and then he turned his attention on to the two young men who were busy giving their official statements to the police after bravely bringing down and restraining the shooter of me before he could kill anyone else. The girlfriend of one of them had actually filmed the whole incident on her Mobil phone which would help the police to investigate and bring charges.

The next thing that I can remember is waking up in a small room surrounded by people in and out of police uniforms and Jane with her head rested upon my chest crying her sweet eyes out. John had told the hospital staff to place me into a private room with two armed police officers on guard. "Jane my darling, where am I, what's happened and why?" were the first words that I spoke once awake and seeing her crying.

On hearing my voice Jane lifted herself back to standing with a look of surprise and adulation that I hadn't seen since the birth of Faith before answering with, "We just saw you shot dead Mike you're alive again but how and why". "I know my love, I've been sent back to do something but I do not know yet" I told her unsure of almost everything. "I need to talk with John my love can you call him babe?" Even before I could finish talking John who was standing back from us said, "I'm right here with you my friend, what can I do." Still uncertain as to what lay ahead of us I firstly needed to know everything possible about any witnesses to what had happened and the guy who had appeared to have just murdered me.

John got onto his walkie talkie and asked whoever was at the other end to bring them to the hospital to help with his inquires and about 30 minutes later the door opened and an officer directed the two brave young men who had probably saved lives by their quick action. At first sight of me not dead as they seen laid out on the street but sat up and alive they both stepped back and looked at each other not believing what they were seeing before them.

"How is this possible?" stammered out one of them "You were shot, we saw it happen." "Errr you're right I was dead but now I'm back." I confirmed. Shocked both of the men had to sit down and steady themselves before another word could be spoken. At that moment the door was pushed open by an official pulling a mobile unit holding a TV and video player. "Sir please forgive my interruption but I think you need to see this."

Once connected to the mains he pushed play and we all watched as the recorded footage of earlier showed everything that happened. It began as the holder was recording her boyfriend and his mate sitting outside of the small cafe on our main street enjoying a hot drink and cigarette like Jane and I often did. "Look at the figure crouching down behind them taking something out of the sports bag he has, and note the clear blue sky with no clouds anywhere. Note the man has a dark shadow around him but nowhere else. I looked at Jane and she at me as if we both knew the cause of it.

The next thing to see was the man pulling out an AK47 gun and aiming it right at me and fired it. The woman holding her Mobil turned in our direction in time to catch me falling forward clutching my stomach before returning to her boyfriend and mate who without hesitation sprung to their feet and very quickly disarmed the unshaven, dark haired shooter and restrained him. When the girlfriend turned her phone back in our direction it plainly showed the bullet hole in my shirt and the blood that was flowing out of me, but it didn't end there as we all could see.

All around there was panic in the street with the screams of the pedestrians and screeching tyres of cars braking as it happened. As I lay there now dead around me there was a glow of brilliant white light and all the blood that had been flowing out of my wound started to go back into my body as the bullet that had just killed me fell out onto the pavement. John straight away looking directly at the two men and said, "Well gentlemen you have just seen exactly the same thing that we have and I am asking you to never tell anyone what you saw, not even your other halves any of this gets out it would create nothing but trouble. There must have a reason for this and I will work with Mike to discover it. If I have to do you mind my contacting you?"

Once Jane and were alone again she asked me what actually happened during the brief time that I was dead as I believe that she knew inside that there was more to it than I had told. I placed my arm around her and recounted that I could remember about my experience. "The figure that sent you back to me would have been your guardian angel, he does what God tells him to do so God must need you for something important.

"Yeah" I said "But how are we going to explain away my miraculous recovery to everyone?". "I'll tell you what to say" came the voice from out of nowhere as the shape of I think my guardian angel slowly appeared in front of us with a strong smell of Lilac. "I have been sent to guide and help you to prevent the devil taking human souls by stopping the wrongs from being carried out in the first place. It is going to be a very hard and testing service that has been appointed to you so you had better get ready. Oh and you can call me Tabec" "One question I have to ask. That is how we can help people overseas." "There are already chosen people where needed." was the reply which helped us both.

After receiving an official discharge from the hospital we were met by a journalist looking for a story for his newspaper concerning my shooting. I was just about to try and excuse it away when as if by magic I felt the weight of something in my pocket which on taking it out revealed a pocket radio complete with a bullet lodged in it as reason for my being alive. After giving a quick story to satisfy the journalist we made our way to the safety and comfort of our home before calling John to have Faith brought back to us.

As everything turned out John managed to lose the film footage and put out the story that I was saved by my Walkman, which had stopped bullet and was able to return home again because the shooter had been caught and arrested by the police. This was enough to satisfy even the many witnesses who had actually been present.

For Jane, Faith and I we were just three people that were in the wrong place at the wrong time and soon enough all was forgotten about enabling us to get on with our lives. That is until Tabec interrupted our lunchtime meal with a mission.